a piece of land *a house with three rooms* *a donkey* *walk into the desert*

[clay relief showing blossoming papyrus, jar stand, and pots of fresh clay]

I made a thing. *My son watched.* *The vizier came.* *It was a good thing.*

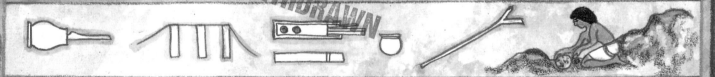

surveying and measuring a monument *from front to back*

chisel *[...king stone]*

[black b...] *...plants of Egypt]*

Senmu... *...sty's heart.*

STORYTELLER'S NOTE

Features blunted by thousands of years, huge paws crumbling, body cracked and sand-scoured, a monument to Khafre, Pharaoh of Egypt, yet endures. Ancient, calm, and noble, staring across the desert to the horizon, it outlasts centuries, and storytellers, too.

ILLUSTRATED BY

DEBORAH NOURSE LATTIMORE

HBJ

HARCOURT BRACE JOVANOVICH, Publishers

San Diego   New York   London

ZEKMET
THE STONE CARVER

A TALE OF ANCIENT EGYPT

BY

MARY STOLZ

Requests for permission to make copies of any part of the work should be mailed to:
Permissions, Harcourt Brace Jovanovich, Publishers, Orlando, Florida 32887.

Library of Congress Cataloging-in-Publication Data
Stolz, Mary, 1920
Zekmet, the stone carver.
Summary: Chosen to design a magnificent monument for a vain and demanding Pharaoh,
an Egyptian stone carver conceives of and begins work on the Sphinx which still stands in
the Egyptian desert today.
[1. Egypt—Civilization—To 332 B.C.—Fiction. 2. Stone carvers—Fiction]
I. Lattimore, Deborah Nourse, ill. II. Title.
PZ7.S875854Ze 1988   [E]   86-22931
ISBN 0-15-299961-2

First edition

A B C D E

The illustrations in this book were done in Winsor & Newton watercolors,
overlaid with Berol Prismacolor pencils on 90-lb. D'Arches hot-press paper stained with
Winsor & Newton watercolors applied in two layers with an elephant-ear sponge
and tissues, and then hand-rubbed and dusted with ponce.
The text type was set in Trump Mediaeval by Thompson Type.
The display type was hand-lettered by the artist.
Printed and bound by South China Printing Company, Quarry Bay, Hong Kong
Designed by Dalia Hartman
Production supervision by Warren Wallerstein and Rebecca Miller

A note about the endpapers: Images on endpapers are taken from text borders, some of which retell
the story in hieroglyphs. Translations of the hieroglyphs appear below each line. Bracketed text
describes images that are not hieroglyphic.

For the sons of Eileen and Robert
Steven, Emmett, Eric
and their wives
Jeanie, Colette, Janet.
With love
—M. S.

For Steve
—D. N. L.

Khafre, Pharaoh of Egypt, ruler of the world, walked with his vizier in the royal gardens, under the blossoming fig trees, beside the reflecting pools.

"Ho-tep," said Pharaoh, "my supreme majesty wishes to have built a monument that will mark, till the end of the world, my exalted role as Ra, the sun god on earth."

"Sire," said Ho-tep, "for many years many laborers have been building your sacred pyramid. In less than a moon, it will be completed. Is that not enough?"

Khafre's cold eyes fixed upon the vizier, who trembled and fell to his knees.

"Your pardon, Majesty. My tongue—it spoke without my knowledge!"

"Teach your tongue a lesson," said Khafre, "or next time I'll cut it out."

"Yes, yes, Exalted One. Your forgiveness is divine."

"Everything about me is divine," said Pharaoh.

Ho-tep put his forehead to the ground in agreement. "Permit me to know what *sort* of monument is in your all-merciful mind," he said as he groveled.

"I have said! One that will honor me forever!"

"But—a shape? You have a vision of what form your illustrious monument should take?"

"Ho-tep, my mind is divinely empty. It is *your* business to think. Bring me a plan tomorrow."

"Tomorrow?" Ho-tep whispered. "Yes, yes. Of course. Tomorrow, Sire."

Khafre motioned with a bejeweled hand. "My majesty is weary of his vizier. Go!"

Ho-tep walked backward from the perfect and perfumed Presence, bowing. He walked out of the palace gates, beyond the palace walls, into the desert.

Soon he came to the workmen's quarters, acres of narrow streets and small mud huts where the laborers who worked on the pyramids lived.

"A monument, a monument," Ho-tep muttered to himself as he stumped across the scorching sands. With his pyramid tomb all but accomplished, Khafre was asking for yet another symbol of deathless splendor.

The greed of pharaohs passed understanding.

"A monument," said Ho-tep desperately. "What more in the way of monuments does the colossal fool want?"

"What colossal fool?"

A young man, sitting on his doorstep, fiddling with a bit of clay, had spoken. A young boy played nearby.

"*How dare you address me?*" said the vizier. His tongue! Would he never learn to keep his tongue locked up?

"Are you someone too important to address?" asked the young man.

"Slave! I am *Ho-tep!*"

"Ah! Then you are important indeed. I am Zekmet. Stone carver, not slave. This is my son, Senmut."

"Do not presume to introduce me to your son, peasant!"

About to call his guard to arrest this rude fellow, Ho-tep instead stayed a moment. "You say you are a stone carver. Are you a good one?"

"The best," said the young man.

"If your carving is as good as your manners are bad, you should be what you say. What is that you have in your hand?"

"It is nothing. A toy," said Zekmet. "I am making it for my son."

"Let me see it," Ho-tep commanded.

Zekmet, who was proud, but merely a stone carver, handed over the toy.

"Ah!" Ho-tep caught his breath as he examined the little clay figure of a donkey carrying sacks of grain. Exquisite. A lovely piece of work.

He handed it back, as if not impressed.

"Have you done other work? Samples I might examine."

Zekmet rose. "If you will follow me, Your Honor."

He led the way to Khafre's pyramid.

A stela at the western entrance depicted Khafre seated on his throne, receiving gifts from a conquered king who crouched at his feet. Two slaves stood behind him with feather fans. In the background geese flew over a bed of rushes.

Ho-tep stared in amazement. Magnificent! What a superb choice of subject! He said, "Who told you what to carve?"

"No one, Your Honor. I was given the slab of marble and told to carve a suitable scene."

"I see." Ho-tep studied the stela, the sky, the distant desert dunes, the stela again. At length he said, "Stone carver, I am about to make you a particular mark of favor."

Zekmet bowed and waited.

"His supreme majesty, exalted Khafre, representative of Ra on earth, wishes to have a monument created in his honor."

Zekmet looked at the pyramid rising to the heavens, fine white limestone casing agleam in the sun, its surmounting cone a blaze of gold.

"He wants still another one," Ho-tep said irritably. He added in haste, "We must insure that coming generations look back upon his reign with wonder. Until the end of the world."

Zekmet waited.

Drawing a deep breath, Ho-tep said, "Zekmet, I am going to permit you to put an idea in my head."

"If it is possible," said Zekmet, "I should be honored."

Ho-tep looked at the stone carver suspiciously. Was this low fellow making sport of him? Whipping was called for!

But then what would he do? While he could not think of a single idea to present to Pharaoh in the morning, he felt that this impudent fellow could come up with a score of notions.

More importantly, he could translate them into stone.

And Zekmet, Ho-tep knew, would never have Khafre's ear, would never even be in the divine presence. Whatever concept Zekmet devised, it would be Ho-tep that Pharaoh would thank. And praise. And *reward*.

"Come," he said to the stone carver. "Draw aside with me. What I have to say is of the utmost secrecy and importance, never to be repeated to a single soul, upon pain of your life."

That evening, sitting outside their mud hut with his wife, Mery-ti, Zekmet said, "So, since he has no ideas of his own and must come up with one quick-quick, my particular mark of favor is to think of an idea for him."

"And what do *we* get out of it?" Mery-ti asked. "Besides a mark of favor."

Zekmet smiled broadly. "At first, he thought that I'd be happy with the honor of serving Pharaoh."

They laughed together.

How Ho-tep would have shuddered at their laughter, their insolence.

"We are to have," Zekmet continued, "a farm of one-quarter of a hectare of good black earth, a house of mud bricks with three rooms, *and* a donkey."

Mery-ti threw her arms about her clever husband.

After a while, she said, "Do you *have* an idea to put in the vizier's head?"

"Not yet," said Zekmet. "I want it to be something strange and wonderful. I want it to be a work of art that will last till the end of the world! Oh, I am as bad as Pharaoh himself, clutching at immortality."

He drew her to her feet. "Come, let us take Senmut and walk out into the desert."

The little family strolled away from the mean streets of workers' hovels into the moonlit desert, where the great black shadow of the king's pyramid fell across sparkling sands. They did not stray far, since wild animals took the desert for their own at night.

"Here," said Zekmet, when they arrived at a small grove of palm trees. "Let us sit and contemplate the night sky, searching for messages from Thoth, moon god and scribe."

Senmut looked at his father with wonder as Zekmet's eyes read the sky from horizon to horizon.

Suddenly, Zekmet held his hand up and whispered, "Hush. Do not move." He pointed toward the pyramid of Khafre, shining under the starry sky.

A lion had appeared out of the dark, intent on some great and secret cat errand. For a moment he was silhouetted against the white limestone monument. He stood with his head up, listening, listening. His face, surrounded by its great mane, turned toward the family under the palm trees.

"Be perfectly still," Zekmet warned in a low voice. "He will not harm us."

For a long time, unmoving, the lion and the peasants faced one another in silence. Then the huge cat glided away, disappearing into the desert.

"A magnificent sight," said Zekmet, illuminated with an idea he dared not utter—so wondrous, so—so *monumental*, he told himself.

Long after his wife and son were asleep on their straw mats, Zekmet sat alone with his idea, trembling with awe.

A concept so massive had never occurred to him before tonight. Yet now it seemed that it had been waiting, all these years, until he and the time and the kingly beast of the desert came together at once.

The next day he took a weighty mass of Nile clay and began to fashion a model of a crouching lion.

When Ho-tep came by in the late morning, he looked upon this figure with displeasure.

"Zekmet! Are you making another toy for your son? I'll have you in chains!"

"Sit down," Zekmet said carelessly, intent on his work. "I'll explain what I am doing."

Ho-tep, who had never had anyone except Khafre himself speak to him in so lofty a tone, considered calling the guard and then sat. This peasant carver was his only hope of satisfying Pharaoh.

"If I had anyone else who could do this," he muttered.

Zekmet smiled. "When you learn what I propose, Ho-tep, you will want to give me a palace!"

"By Bes, when I want to give you a palace, you worm, the sun will collide with the moon!"

Zekmet turned his model toward the vizier, who stared at what he saw. "But this is—this is—"

"A model, Your Honor. A small model of the monument I propose."

"It's a lion!"

"A lion. The kingliest of beasts, with the face of the kingliest of Pharaohs."

Ho-tep leaned forward. "It is," he breathed. "It is, indeed, a superb lion with a man's face! It bears the royal uraeus of divine kingship. I have never before seen its like!"

"There has never been its like until now," Zekmet said proudly.

Still Ho-tep stared. "That face. One cannot, in truth, say it is a *perfect* likeness of Khafre, the earthly sun god."

"I did not think his sacred majesty would wish to go down through the ages with his own features. Perhaps when he was young he was handsomer."

Ho-tep stroked his chin. It was true. To put, on this noble beast, Khafre's face, wrinkled and hard-featured, would not please the royal eye. Not that Khafre at any age had looked like this.

"Your son," Ho-tep said, thinking back. "I believe I detect something of him in this. Is it, just possibly, sacrilege?"

But he pondered. Peasant offspring Senmut was, but handsome of face. With the royal uraeus, which Zekmet had carefully placed on the elegant head, this was a countenance of which any ruler could be proud. In this likeness, Khafre would be dazzling in men's eyes for all ages to come.

"What size have you in mind for this monument, Zekmet?"
Ho-tep asked. "And of what material will you build it? Shall we
have to quarry the western hills for limestone?"

"No, Your Honor. Last night I studied the area surrounding
the pyramid of Khafre and found great granite outcroppings. I
shall carve directly in the rock."

"What size?" Ho-tep whispered hoarsely.

"I paced three hundred feet. Allowing for loss in the carving, I

believe the monument will measure over two hundred feet from haunch to forepaw when completed. It will rise over one hundred feet from the desert floor, dominating earth and sky."

Ho-tep knew that when Pharaoh saw this model and heard how large, how majestic a monument was to be created, he would be elated. He would bestow vast rewards upon his vizier, the adviser who had thought of such a memorial to his majesty and power.

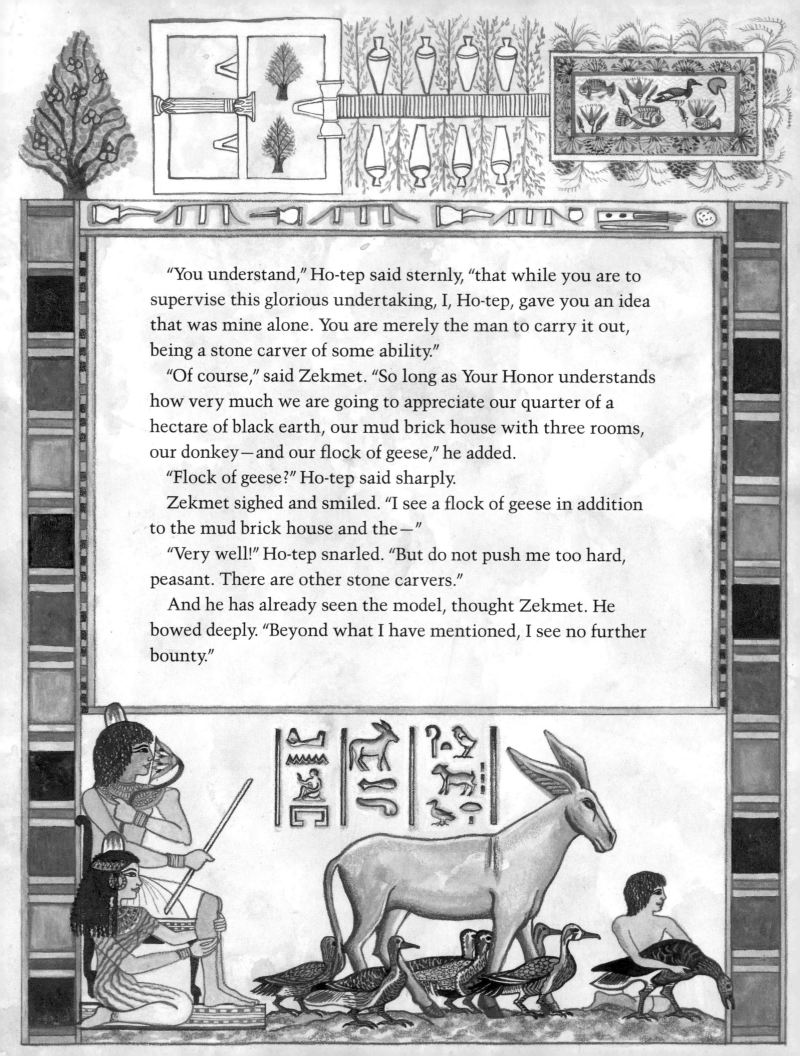

"You understand," Ho-tep said sternly, "that while you are to supervise this glorious undertaking, I, Ho-tep, gave you an idea that was mine alone. You are merely the man to carry it out, being a stone carver of some ability."

"Of course," said Zekmet. "So long as Your Honor understands how very much we are going to appreciate our quarter of a hectare of black earth, our mud brick house with three rooms, our donkey—and our flock of geese," he added.

"Flock of geese?" Ho-tep said sharply.

Zekmet sighed and smiled. "I see a flock of geese in addition to the mud brick house and the—"

"Very well!" Ho-tep snarled. "But do not push me too hard, peasant. There are other stone carvers."

And he has already seen the model, thought Zekmet. He bowed deeply. "Beyond what I have mentioned, I see no further bounty."

"Good," said Ho-tep, reaching for the clay model. "I shall show this to his divine majesty and let you know the answer by tomorrow. One thing further—how long will it take to complete this great stone carving?"

"That will depend upon how many workmen I am allowed," replied Zekmet.

"As many as you need," Ho-tep said.

"Then—perhaps ten years?"

"But great Khafre will be dead in ten years! He wants *all* his monuments completed before he dies!"

Zekmet shrugged. Peasants and pharaohs had but one thing in common. None could stay the moment of death.

"He will see the work as it progresses, and know that his great stone image will guard his pyramid and reign over the desert throughout eternity. I fear even Pharaoh must rest content with that."

Khafre was pleased almost past words with the vision his excellent vizier presented to him.

"My majesty had no notion that his vizier would actually find an idea in a mere night's thinking, Ho-tep," he said. "You have surpassed anything I believed you capable of."

Ho-tep inclined his head modestly. "I was inspired by your bliss-giving need for yet another—that is, for a monument that would honor you till the end of time."

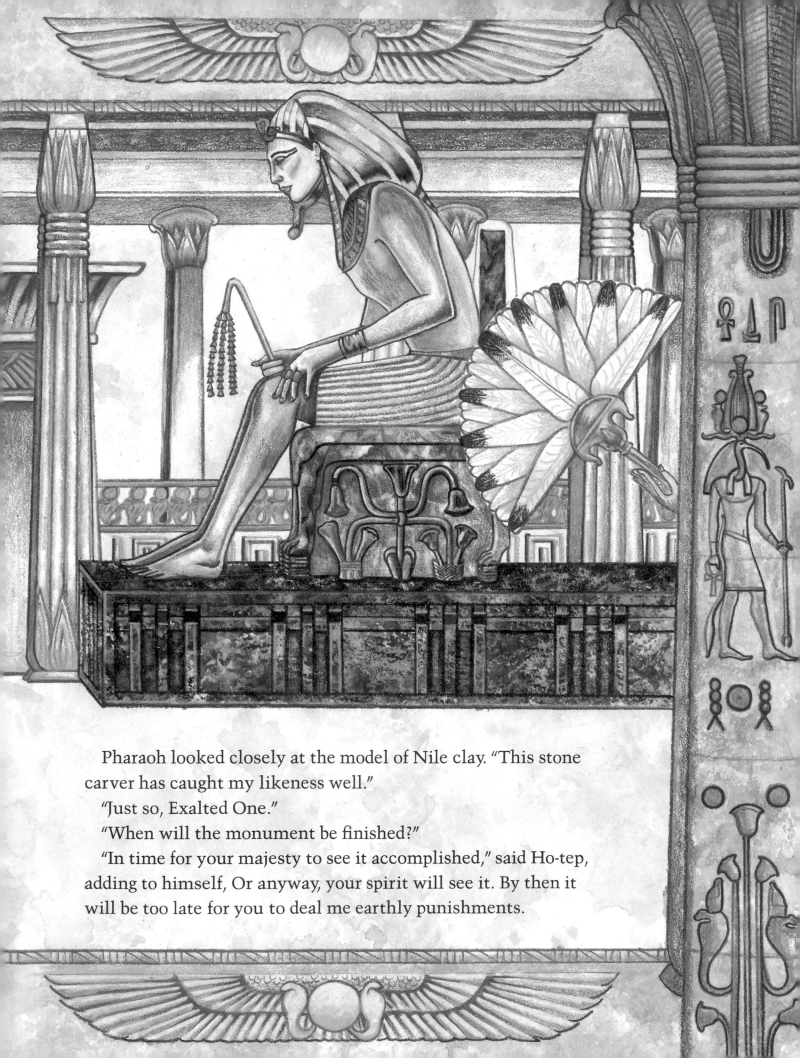

Pharaoh looked closely at the model of Nile clay. "This stone carver has caught my likeness well."

"Just so, Exalted One."

"When will the monument be finished?"

"In time for your majesty to see it accomplished," said Ho-tep, adding to himself, Or anyway, your spirit will see it. By then it will be too late for you to deal me earthly punishments.

Khafre did not live to see the fulfillment of his last memorial,
the great lion image that still rises from the desert floor in front
of his pyramid tomb.

It was Senmut, son of Zekmet, who completed the work—
Senmut, by then the most renowned of all the sculptors of
Egypt.

One day he stood back and said to his workmen, "We have created!" And he sent up a prayer of love and praise to his father, Zekmet, gone west like Pharaoh himself.

If it did not happen that way, it happened some other way.
For the sphinx still stands, great against the blue Egyptian sky.
It will be there tomorrow, and tomorrow. . . .

Khafre,   son of Ra   the two ladies   King of Upper and Lower Egypt   the golden Horus in the sky

Zekmet, the stone carver   his majesty   life   health   the good
                                                   prosperity   stability   god

They spoke.   Isis   Osiris   Horus   Hathor   [making an offering]   [threshing grain]   Nepthys

H'py, the Nile god   Geb, the Earth god   [making mud brick]

proceed   offering   made to the lord of the two lands   in his image   before his pyramid

[Horus, the living pharaoh, crossing the morning sky in his sun bark]

[Thoth, god of learning and of the moon, crossing the night sky in his lunar bark]